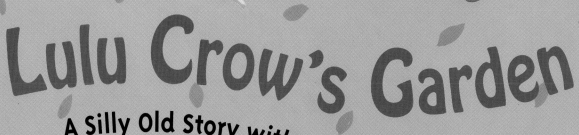

Lulu Crow's Garden

A Silly Old Story with Brand-New Pictures

by Lizi Boyd

Little, Brown and Company
Boston   New York   Toronto   London

To Sally and her gardens
at Teel Cove Farm

First Edition

Library of Congress Cataloging-in-Publication Data

Boyd, Lizi
    Lulu Crow's garden : a silly old story with brand-new
pictures / by Lizi Boyd. — 1st ed.
        p.   cm.
    Based on the picture book Johnny Crow's garden by
L. Leslie Brooke published in 1903.
    Summary: Rhyming nonsense verses picture Lulu Crow in
her garden with all her animal friends.
    ISBN 0-316-10419-1
    [1. Crows — Fiction.   2. Animals — Fiction.   3. Gardens —
Fiction.   4. Stories in rhyme.]   I. Brooke, L. Leslie
(Leonard Leslie) 1862—1940   Johnny Crow's garden.   II. Title.
    PZ8.3.B6885Lu   1998
    [E] — dc21   96-49012

10 9 8 7 6 5 4 3 2 1

SC

Published simultaneously in Canada by Little, Brown & Company
(Canada) Limited

$14.45   3-98

Printed in Hong Kong

The paintings for this book were done in gouache on Strathmore Bristol paper.
The display type was set in Hobo. The text type was set in Triplex Bold.

JP
BOY
C.2

This way to Lulu Crow's Garden.

Lulu Crow
Would dig and sow

Till she made a little Garden.

And the Lion

Had a green-and-yellow Tie on

In Lulu Crow's Garden.

And the Rat
Wore a Feather in his Hat.

But the Bear
Had nothing to wear

In Lulu Crow's Garden.

So the Ape

Took his Measure with a Tape.

Then the Crane

Was caught in the Rain.

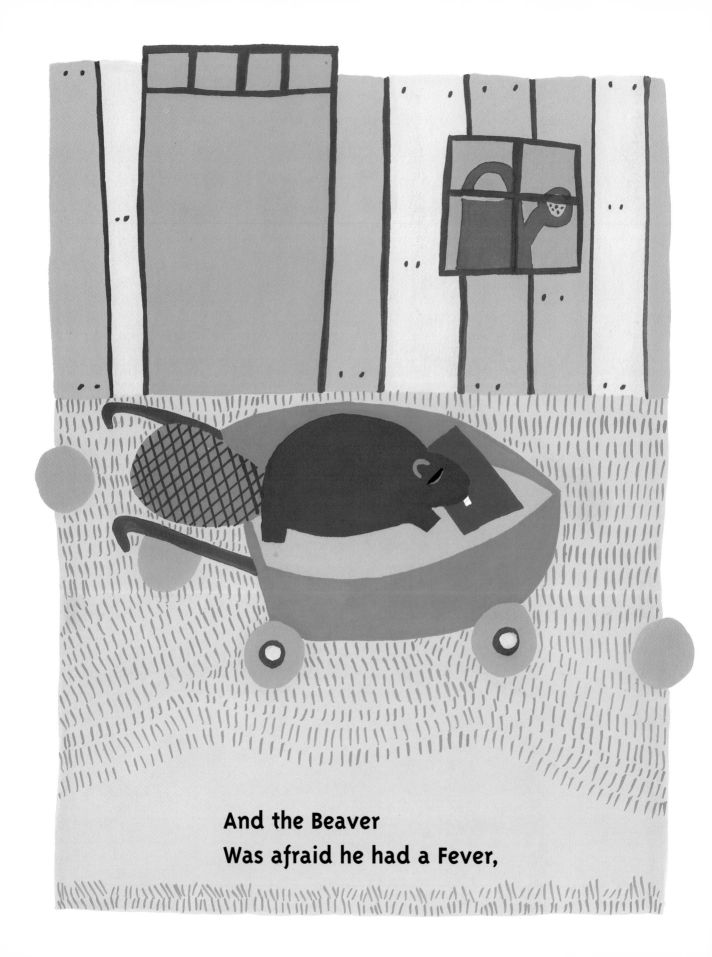

And the Beaver
Was afraid he had a Fever,

But the Goat said,
"It's nothing but his Throat!"

So the Pig danced a Jig.

And the Goose

Was just a Goose.

And the Mouse

Built a House,

Where the Cat sat on a Mat

In Lulu Crow's Garden.

And the Whale

Told a very long Tale.

Then the Red Fox

Put them in a Blue Box

Till Lulu Crow let them go.

And they all sat down to dinner in one big Row